To the strong women in my life, mi mamá, mi tía, y mi abuela—
muchisimas gracias for making my life deliciosa!—M.G.

To mis abuelitas, Carlota y Margarita, and to all the abuelitas
near and far who passed love through their delicious recipes.—L.L.

Book design by Melissa Nelson Greenberg

Published in 2021 by CAMERON + COMPANY, a division of ABRAMS.

Library of Congress Cataloging-in-Publication Data available.
ISBN: 978-1-951836-22-1

Printed in China

10 9 8 7 6 5 4 3

CAMERON KIDS is an imprint of CAMERON + COMPANY

CAMERON + COMPANY
Petaluma, California
www.cameronbooks.com

MAY YOUR LIFE BE DELICIOSA

Michael Genhart • Loris Lora

cameron kids

Every year on Christmas Eve, my abuela Pina, mamá, tía, sister, cousins, and I gather in Abuela's kitchen to make tamales.

¡Es una tamalada! A party in the kitchen!

Music playing. Feet dancing. Voices singing. Storytelling.

It's also a lot of work. Everyone has a job to do.

My sister, Pancha, and I soak and clean the corn husks in warm water, making sure to remove the silk threads.

My cousins chop onions and garlic, trying not to tear up.

My tía roasts the chiles.

Mamá prepares the corn masa dough,
mixing it with lard and the roasted chiles.

And Abuela is in charge of cooking the meat
filling, with its secret seasonings.

"Where is the recipe?" I ask. Abuela laughs.

"It is in my heart, Rosie. I use mis ojos, my eyes, to measure.
Mis manos, my hands, to feel. Mi boca, my mouth, to taste.

My abuela gave it to me and I am giving it to you."

My favorite part is when Abuela tells us how to make a tamale.

We already know how. We do it every year.

It's Abuela's stories we love to hear again and again.

When it's time, I shout,
         "¡Abuela Pina, cuéntanos, por favor!"

And so she begins.

"You start with una hoja, a corn husk. The warm water has made it softer and easier to work with."

Abuela looks into my eyes and smiles. "Rosie, mi nieta, may you always be flexible."

Flexible

Abuela takes the husk, the outer part of the tamale,
and says, "May you always have protection and security."

Protección y
Seguridad

She applies the dough to the husk—not too thick and not too thin. She explains, "La masa comes from corn. Like a cornstalk, may you always stand tall and proud."

Then Abuela adds the meat filling with roasted chiles. "May you always have food to eat and spice to make things special."

Comida suficiente y bien condimentada

And then she adds an olive, placing it right at the heart of the tamale. "May you have love and affection in your life always."

Amor y cariño

Abuela carefully folds the tamale, bringing one side toward the center, then the other, before folding the bottom upward. "May you have lots and lots of hugs."

muchos abrazos

She places the tamale in a large pot, one leaning upon the other.
"May you always have the support of family and community."

Familia y
Comunidad

Now it's my turn. With Abuela's wishes in my heart, I take my place in the kitchen, and shoulder to shoulder, we all make dozens and dozens of tamales.

We soak the husk, warm and soft.

We spread the masa and stand up tall.

We add the meat and hear our stomachs growl.

We hide the olive and dream of love.

We fold them snug like Abuela's hugs.

I don't need a recipe. I use my eyes to measure, my hands to feel, my mouth to taste.

And then we wait for the tamales to steam, their delicious scent filling the air.

Abuela reminds us all, "May you always have patience with yourself and others."

Paciencia

We groan. A few hours feels like a lifetime.

But then it's time to eat. We carefully unwrap the tamales one by one.

¡Deliciosa!

"May your life be delicious!" Abuela sings.

Every Christmas Eve we gather,
year after year after year . . .

And now I give to you what my abuela gave to me.
"You start with una hoja . . ."

AUTHOR'S NOTE

ROSITA CASTRO, AUTHOR'S MOTHER, THE ORIGINAL ROSIE

THE AUTHOR, HIS ABUELA, AND MAMÁ ROSITA

I have fond memories growing up in the 1960s and '70s in Southern California, where homes were surrounded by large fields of strawberries, lima beans, walnuts, and oranges—the very fields where members of my family worked picking produce or in the packinghouses where it was boxed and shipped. We lived among a fairly large Latinx community, a community very proud of its heritage and culture. Making tamales was an important part of this culture, our culture.

As the only boy in the kitchen, surrounded by all of the women in my family, I felt the excitement of helping make tamales every Christmas Eve. I was both an observer and a participant, watching every detail and working alongside everyone else. There was nowhere else I wanted to be on this day, the kitchen buzzing with activity. In the background played the ranchera music of my mother's childhood, and my grandmother, mother, and aunt sang and danced along.

What captivated me the most were the stories. My grandmother recounted tales of her childhood, some of which were passed on to her from her mother and grandmother. Stories of hardship, stories of joy, and stories that seemed fantastic to me. Some made us laugh out loud, and some scared us—like the stories of ghosts or fantasmas that drew us all in but also spooked us.

I loved being a part of this family tradición and ritual that had long preceded me, knowing it would continue long after me. I felt the richness of the spoken word and the importance of an oral history that passed from one generation to the next— storytelling that connected family over time, and memories or recuerdos that linked the oldest family members to the youngest ones.

Each story seemed to contain some kind of message about living one's life fully. *May Your Life Be Deliciosa* illustrates the tenor of many of these stories and the themes that ran through so many of them—themes of love, support, and togetherness. I think every family has stories to tell and share across generations. I hope this book inspires and encourages young children to ask their parents and grandparents about such stories, so they can then pass them on to their children and grandchildren. Storytelling connects us all.

ILLUSTRATOR'S NOTE

The illustrations created for *May Your Life Be Deliciosa* were inspired by the rich tamale-making traditions of my Mexican family and the many generations before us. While working on this book, I found myself fondly reflecting on past holiday memories. I grew up in a Southern California Mexican household and Christmastime always felt so colorful to me, with its sparkling decorations and plentiful amounts of delicious cuisine. Colorful foods and drinks like tamales, pozole, buñuelos, atole, and ponche created a comforting smell that filled our tiny house.

The holidays were always a big celebration at my home. Friends and family, both young and old, gathered to prepare tamales together. I personally loved learning how to spread masa onto a warm husk and adding just the right amount of salsa before quickly folding and adding it to a tray of what felt like a million other tamales.

I wanted to capture that warm essence of family, food, and togetherness on each page with the hope that others can relate to it as well.

THE ILLUSTRATOR (SECOND FROM LEFT), HER SIBLINGS AND COUSINS, WITH THEIR ABUELITA, CARLOTTA, IN MEXICO.